Contents

SNOW!

CHAPTER 1

Bertie woke up. He pulled back the curtains and gasped. SNOW! For weeks he'd been praying for snow and now it had finally come. Whoopee! Snowmen! Snowball fights! And even better, sledging on Pudsley Hill!

He burst into his parents' bedroom. "IT'S SNOWING!" he yelled.

"Uhh … what?" mumbled Mum.

"It's snowing! Look outside!" shouted Bertie, pulling back the curtains.

Dad squinted at the alarm clock and groaned. "Bertie, it's not even six o'clock!"

"But it's snowing!" said Bertie.

"I don't care – go back to bed!"

Bertie went. A moment later his head poked round the door. "Do you think school will be closed?" he asked.

"BACK TO BED!" bellowed Dad.

But Bertie was too excited – how could anyone sleep when it was snowing outside? He hurried downstairs.

"Hey, Whiffer! Look, it's snowing!"

They stood at the window watching the snow coming down. There was snow on the rooftops and snow carpeting the lawn. Bertie looked at Whiffer…

Dirty Bertie

Five minutes later they were in the garden. Bertie bounded around, chased excitedly by Whiffer. Snowflakes fell on his face and melted on his tongue. He scooped up a big ball of snow. *If only Darren and Eugene were here*, he thought, *we could have a snowball fight.*

CRUMP! His snowball thudded against the side of the shed.

"BERTIE!"

Uh oh. Mum stuck her head out of the back door.

"What on earth are you doing?" she cried.

"Playing," replied Bertie.

"You're still in your pyjamas! They'll get soaked!"

Bertie looked down. It was true, his pyjamas had got a little bit soggy.

"I'm wearing boots," he said.

"For heaven's sake, come in before you catch your death!"

Bertie drooped inside, trailing wet footprints through the kitchen. Whiffer shook himself, showering snow everywhere.

"Ugh!" said Mum. "Look at you, Bertie, you're wet through!"

"It's only snow," said Bertie.

"Go and get some clothes on."

In his bedroom Bertie quickly pulled on his jeans and thumped downstairs.

The phone was ringing in the hall.

"Yes?" he said, snatching up the receiver.

"Hey, Bertie!" It was Darren. "Have you heard? School's closed!"

Dirty Bertie

Bertie did a wild dance of joy. "We can have snowball fights!" he whooped.

"And go sledging!" cried Darren.

"I'll meet you at Pudsley Hill," said Bertie. "Tell Eugene."

"Okay. Bring your sledge!" said Darren.

Bertie slammed down the phone. This was going to be the greatest day ever. No school, no mean old Miss Boot – he could spend the whole day playing in the snow. Wait a moment, though. Bertie gulped. Didn't his sledge accidentally get broken last year when they tried it with four people? Argh! Disaster! He had to find a sledge and fast.

Dirty Bertie

"Guess what? School's closed!" cried Bertie, scooting into the kitchen.

Dad groaned. Suzy cheered.

"Can I go sledging with my friends?" asked Bertie.

Mum sighed. "After breakfast."

"And can we get a new sledge?"

"Certainly not," said Dad.

"But ours is broken!" moaned Bertie.

"And whose fault is that?" said Mum.

"It wasn't mine. I *told* Darren he was too heavy."

"Well, we're not wasting money on sledges so you can break them," said Mum. "If you're that desperate, go and ask your gran."

"Why, is she going sledging?"

"I mean, ask if she's got a sledge. I'm sure she used to have one."

CHAPTER 2

Gran was still in her dressing gown
when Bertie knocked on her door.

"Bertie!" she said. "Shouldn't you be at
school?"

"SCHOOL'S CLOSED!" whooped
Bertie. "IT'S SNOWING!"

"So I see," said Gran. "You'd better
come in."

Dirty Bertie

Bertie stamped his boots on the mat. "I've got the whole day off," he panted. "And me and my friends are going sledging, only there's one problem – we don't have a sledge."

"Oh dear," said Gran. "So what are you going to do?"

"I was hoping you'd got one," said Bertie.

"A sledge?" Gran frowned. "I think I did have one somewhere. It belonged to your dad."

"But you kept it?" asked Bertie hopefully.

"Well, I don't remember throwing it out."

"Great! Then can I borrow it – I mean, if you're not using it?"

Gran smiled. "I'm not right now,"

she said. "Wait while I get dressed and we'll have a look in the shed."

Gran's shed was so full of junk it was difficult to get in the door. Bertie stared at the jumble of deckchairs, boxes and rusty lawnmowers. Gran waded in and began to hunt through the piles of stuff. Finally she found what she was looking for.

"There! I knew it was here somewhere," she said.

Bertie stared, boggle-eyed. The sledge looked like something out of the Stone Age! It was made of heavy planks of wood nailed together. At the front was a bit of knotted old rope for steering. It smelled of mould.

"Your dad used to love this sledge!" said Gran, brushing off a cobweb.

"Really?" said Bertie. In the old days
sledges must have been rubbish. Today
they were light and fast, and you didn't
need a team of huskies to pull them.

"What do you think?" said Gran.

"Oh, um … yeah. Thanks, Gran!" said
Bertie, trying to sound enthusiastic.

At least it was a sledge, and right now
it was better than nothing.

17

Dirty Bertie

Bertie dragged the sledge down the street. By now all his friends would be up at Pudsley Hill. As he turned the corner a boy came out of a shop with his mum, pulling a sledge behind him. Bertie's heart sank. It was Know-All Nick – the last person on earth he wanted to see.

"Oh, hello, Bertie!" he sneered.

"Hello," said Bertie coldly.

Bertie had never met Nick's mum before. She looked exactly like him, pale and neat with a long, snooty nose. She stared at Bertie as if he had fleas.

"And who is this, Nicholas?" she said. "One of your school-friends?"

"No, this is Bertie," said Nick with a sickly grin. "Going to Pudsley Hill?"

Dirty Bertie

"I might be," said Bertie.

"I've got a new sledge," boasted Nick. "It's a Speedster 2000. Isn't it a beauty?"

Bertie stared. It was the sledge of his dreams – curved and sleek, with steel runners and go-faster stripes down the side. Trust Nick to have the best sledge you could buy.

"Mummy said I could have any one I liked, didn't you, Mummy?" he simpered.

"Of course I did, bunnikins."

Nick flushed pink.

"Anyway, I better be going," said Bertie. "My friends will be waiting for me."

"Yes, come along, Nicholas," said Nick's mum. But Nick had other ideas.

"HA HA!" he hooted. "IS THAT YOUR SLEDGE?"

Bertie scowled. "It's my gran's. And it's faster than it looks."

"Yeah?" said Nick. "Where did you get it from – a joke shop?"

"Don't be rude, Nicholas," tutted Nick's mum. "Come along."

"Bye, Bertie!" grinned Know-All Nick. "See you on the hill – if your sledge makes it that far!"

CHAPTER 3

By the time Bertie arrived, the hill was packed with children. Screams of laughter rang out. Sledges whizzed down the steep slope.

Eugene and Darren were waiting for him, idly throwing snowballs.

"What kept you so long?" asked Eugene.

21

"And what do you call THAT?" asked Darren.

"A sledge," said Bertie. "I borrowed it from my gran."

"But where's your old one?"

"If you remember, you helped break it," said Bertie. "This is the best I could do."

Darren shook his head. "That's going to be rubbish," he said.

"It smells," said Eugene, holding his nose.

Bertie rolled his eyes. "Well, get your own sledge if you're so fussy!" he said. "Anyway, it's better than it looks."

They tried a practice run. It took both Darren and Eugene to launch the sledge with Bertie on board. It trundled gently at first then gained a little speed, bumping and bouncing down the hill like

Dirty Bertie

an old pram. Bertie clambered off and rubbed his bottom. It was even worse than he'd thought.

"OH, BERTIE! BERTIE!"

Bertie turned round and groaned. That was all he needed – Angela Nicely. Angela lived next door to Bertie and was always telling everyone that he was her boyfriend. She had her friends Laura and Maisie with her.

"Look, Bertie! We're making a snowman!" she sang excitedly.

Dirty Bertie

The snowman had a fat, lumpy body
and was already taller than Angela. It
stood at the foot of the slope, looking
up the hill with its two coal eyes. Sledges
whizzed past on either side.

"You can't build it there!" said Bertie.

"Why not?" said Angela.

"It's in the way!"

"No it's not!"

"Yes it is. We're sledging here," said
Bertie. "You'll have to move it!"

"*You* move," said Angela, sticking out
her tongue. "It's our snowman and we
were here first."

Bertie shrugged. "Okay, but don't say
I didn't warn you."

ZOOOOOM!

Something streaked past
them in a blur of speed.

Dirty Bertie

Know-All Nick skidded to a halt on his Speedster 2000 and got off.

"Whoo-hoo! See that?" he whooped. "That was lightning!"

"We're making a snowman!" cried Angela.

Nick ignored her. "Oh, look, it's Bertie with his grandma's sledge," he jeered.

"Ha ha," said Bertie. "Actually, it's a lot faster than it looks."

Nick smirked. "That old crate?"

"It's better than yours."

"Oh yeah?" Nick folded his arms. "Well, if you're so sure, let's have a race. First one to the bottom of the hill."

Dirty Bertie

"You're on," said Bertie.

Angela clapped her hands. "Goodie! A race! I'll be the judge."

Bertie trudged up the hill, dragging the sledge behind him. He was already wishing he'd kept his big mouth shut. He flopped down on the snow beside Darren and Eugene and told them the bad news.

"A race?" said Eugene. "Are you mad?"

"He was showing off," said Bertie. "What else could I have done?"

"But a race…? Have you *seen* his sledge?"

"Tell him you changed your mind," said Darren.

"I can't, not now," said Bertie. "I'll look stupid."

"You'll look even more stupid when you lose," said Darren.

"You never know," said Bertie. "I *might* win."

"On that old heap?" said Darren. "You'd be faster in a wheelbarrow."

CHAPTER 4

The two sledges lined up at the top of the hill. Word had got round about the Great Sledge Race and a crowd from school gathered to watch. Eugene was in charge of starting the race. At the bottom of the hill, Angela Nicely waited to wave her hanky when the winner crossed the finish.

Dirty Bertie

"Want me to give you a head start, Bertie?" smirked Know-All Nick.

"No thanks," said Bertie.

The two rivals got ready. Bertie lay on his front, to give his sledge extra speed.

Nick sat back on the Speedster 2000, looking smugly confident. This was going to be so easy, he wouldn't even need to cheat. He couldn't wait to see Bertie's face when he beat him by miles.

Bertie gripped the rope tight between his hands. "Ready?" he asked.

"Any time you like, slowcoach," drawled Nick.

Darren crouched down, ready to push Bertie off. Trevor did the same for Nick.

Eugene raised his arm.

"After three," he said. "Three … two … one … GO!"

Darren launched the heavy wooden sledge with all his might. It lurched forward and caught the slope, starting to bump down the hill. Bertie hung on tight. Snow kicked in his face, almost blinding him. But he was in the lead – there was no sign of that show-off Nick. He must have got a slow start.

I can win this, thought Bertie. *Just keep going and…*

WHOOOOOOOOOSH!

Something zoomed past, showering him with snow. Bertie gaped. The Speedster 2000 whizzed down the hill like a rocket-powered missile. Bertie tried to urge Gran's old sledge to go faster, but he might as well have got off and walked.

Dirty Bertie

Nick grinned. The race was in the bag. He was way out in front. He turned round to see how far behind Bertie was.

"What's the matter, loser?" he yelled. "Can't you go—"

WHUMPF!

Nick never saw the giant snowman. One minute he was racing down the hill, and the next he was flying through the air like a human cannonball.

KADOOF! He landed head first in a big pile of snow.

ZOOOOOOM!

Bertie's wooden sledge flew by, passing Angela Nicely and crossing the finish before spinning to a stop.

Bertie jumped off and leaped in the air.

"YES! I WON! I WON!" he yelled.

At the top of the hill Darren, Eugene and the rest of the crowd were cheering.

Bertie hurried over to where Nick was struggling in the snow like a beetle on its back. He pulled him out.

"ARGHH! BLECH!" spluttered Nick, wiping his eyes.

"Oh dear, Nick, you're a bit wet!" Bertie grinned.

33

"YOU CHEATED!" gasped Nick.

Bertie shook his head. "You said first to the bottom of the hill. I was first."

"But … but… IT'S NOT FAIR!" wailed Nick, stamping his foot with rage. "You just wait, I'm going to—"

SPLAT! A big snowball hit Nick right on the ear.

"THAT'S HIM! HE WRECKED OUR SNOWMAN!" yelled Angela Nicely.

"GET HIM!"

SPLAT! SPLAT!

Snowballs pelted Nick from all sides, as Laura and Maisie joined in the attack.

Bertie grinned. There was nothing better than a snowball fight – especially when the target was snooty-nosed Nick.

He stooped down to grab a fistful of snow. It was turning into the perfect day.

CHAPTER 1

Bertie watched his dad through the window. He was marching up and down the garden with a rake over his shoulder.

"What's he doing?" he asked.

Mum rolled her eyes. "Your father's joined the Black-Axe Battle Society. Grown men playing at soldiers. Can you imagine it?"

Bertie could. It sounded brilliant.

"You mean they fight REAL battles?" he said excitedly.

"No!" snorted Mum. "It's all pretend. Running round in silly hats, waving swords."

Bertie watched his dad take aim at a flowerpot. A battle club? Why hadn't anyone told him before? He was brilliant at fighting, and what's more he already had his own pirate costume.

Over supper he tried to find out more about it.

"Dad, you know this battle club you're in?" he said.

"It's not a battle club," said Dad. "It's a historical society."

Dirty Bertie

Mum pulled a face at Suzy.

"But you fight battles?" said Bertie.

"We *stage* battles," corrected Dad. "It's history, Bertie. We bring history to life."

Bertie sucked up a loop of spaghetti. "And you dress up?" he said.

"We wear costumes, yes."

"And fight with swords?"

"Not just swords – we have all kinds of weapons," said Dad.

Bertie thought for a moment. "So if I came, could I be a pirate?"

Dad gave a heavy sigh. "It's nothing to do with pirates, Bertie. It's the English Civil War – the Royalists against the Roundheads."

"Why are they round heads?"

"It's just a nickname. The Royalists were on the King's side, the Roundheads fought against them."

"I'd be on the King's side," decided Bertie. "Actually, I wouldn't mind being King myself."

"You won't be anything because you're not coming," said Dad.

Bertie gaped. "Why not?"

"Yes, why not?" said Mum. "If you can play at soldiers, why can't Bertie?"

"Because it's not a game!" cried Dad crossly. "We train every week like a real army. We have to obey orders."

Dirty Bertie

"We do that at school," said Bertie.

"Anyway, I'm not letting you near a battlefield," said Dad. "There'll be guns and cannons – all kinds of dangerous things."

"Cannons?" gasped Bertie. "Brilliant! *Please* can I come?"

"No," said Dad firmly. "And don't go on because I won't change my mind."

Mum cleared away the plates. "Well, I think you're being very mean," she sniffed. "Bertie would make a very good pirate."

Dad put his head in his hands. "IT'S NOTHING TO DO WITH PIRATES!"

CHAPTER 2

On Wednesday night Dad went to
battle practice. When he returned, Bertie
was in the lounge watching TV with
Mum and Suzy. Whiffer was sprawled
out on the floor.

There was a clanking in the hall and
Dad appeared in the doorway.

"Well, what do you think?" he said.

Dirty Bertie

"Good grief!" said Mum. "Did you walk home like that?"

Bertie stared. His dad was wearing a tin helmet that looked like a pudding bowl. Long boots flapped around his knees and he seemed to have lost the bottom half of his trousers. In his hand was an enormous pole tipped with a sharp blade.

"Wow! Is that your axe?" said Bertie impressed.

"It's called a pike," said Dad. "I'm a pikeman in the royal army."

Dirty Bertie

"You look like you're in the circus," said Mum. "Be careful with that thing."

"Can I have a go?" begged Bertie.

Dad shook his head. "No, it's not for children."

"Please," said Bertie. "I just want to see what it's like."

"Oh, let him have a go," sighed Mum.

"Well, all right," said Dad, "but just for a moment, and don't go poking anyone in the eye."

Bertie jumped up eagerly. He'd never held a pike before.

Dirty Bertie

It would be brilliant for poking people in the bottom. Know-All Nick for instance.

"Not like that," said Dad. "You need both hands. One up here to steady it. Got it?"

"Yes," said Bertie.

"You're sure?"

"I'm fine!" said Bertie. "Let go!"

Dad let go. The pike was a lot heavier than Bertie had expected. It started to fall.

"LOOK OUT!" cried Mum, ducking out of the way. Bertie heaved and managed to jerk the pole back upright.

CLANG! SMASH! TINKLE!

There was the sound of breaking glass and the light went out. Bertie stumbled over something in the dark, lost his grip on the pike and dropped it with a thump.

WOOF! WOOF!

"BERTIE!" yelled Mum.

"It's all right," cried Bertie. "It's only Whiffer. I trod on his tail."

Once they'd cleared up the bits of glass, Dad replaced the broken light.

"It wasn't my fault!" repeated Bertie for the tenth time.

Mum glared at Dad. "It's you I blame," she said.

"ME?" said Dad.

Dirty Bertie

"It's your stupid spear!"

"It's not a spear," said Dad. "It's a pike."

"I don't care what it is, don't bring it in the house!"

"I've got to practise for Saturday," argued Dad.

"And that's another thing," said Mum. "I'm taking Suzy shopping on Saturday."

Dad's mouth fell open. "But that's the day of my first battle. What about Bertie?"

"I'm not dragging him round the shops with us," said Mum. "Last time I took him to Dibble's, he jumped in a lift and ended up on the fifth floor!"

"Who's going to look after him, then?" asked Dad.

"You are!"

"I can't! I'll be fighting the battle."

"Well, surely Bertie can go and watch?" said Mum.

"Yes! Can I, Dad?" begged Bertie.

Dad looked at him wearily. "If you must," he sighed.

Bertie whooped.

"But you're only coming to watch," warned Dad. "You are NOT taking part."

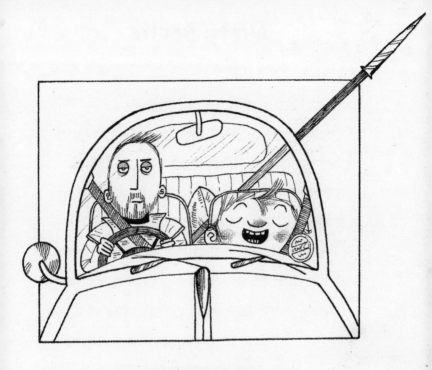

CHAPTER 3

Saturday morning dawned. Bertie chattered excitedly to Dad all the way to the battlefield. When they arrived, he stared … where was the battle? He had expected two great armies with banners and knights in armour. Instead there was a scattering of tents at the foot of a hill. People were strolling around dressed in long boots and floppy hats.

"Right," said Dad, locking the car and heading for a white tent. "You wait outside while I go and sign in. And don't wander off or touch anything."

"I won't," promised Bertie. He stood outside the tent watching some soldiers who were smoking pipes round a fire. After ten minutes he noticed a queue had formed behind him.

"Right, who's next?" asked a big, bearded man, appearing from the tent.

Dirty Bertie

"What's your name, lad?"

"Who me?" said Bertie.

"Well you're in the queue. What's your name?"

"Bertie. Bertie Burns."

The man checked his list. "You're not down here," he said. "Never mind, who are you with?"

"My dad," said Bertie.

"No, I mean whose side are you on? Parliament or the King?"

"Oh, I'm for the King," said Bertie.

"Good lad," said the man. "Well, as it happens, the King's army is short of a drummer boy – how does that sound?"

Bertie's face lit up. "Brilliant. Oh, but I haven't got a drum."

"Don't worry about that," said the man. "Pop into the tent and see Sarah, she'll kit you out with a uniform."

Bertie hurried inside. He couldn't believe his luck. He was actually going to take part in the battle. Wait till his dad heard about this!

A short time later he emerged from the tent wearing a black jacket, a flat hat and baggy velvet bloomers. A large blue drum hung at his side. Bertie banged it a few times to see what kind of noise it made. The soldiers round the fire looked up and glared.

Just then Dad appeared. "Bertie!
Where have you been?" he cried.
He stared. "What's that?"

"It's a drum," said Bertie.

"Yes, but what are you doing with it?"

"I'm a drummer
boy in the army.
Listen to this," said
Bertie.

He played a
deafening drum roll.
BRRRRRRRRRRR…

"STOP!" yelled
Dad. "I thought
I made it clear you
weren't in the battle?"

"It wasn't my fault! They needed a
drummer!" said Bertie.

They were interrupted by a red-faced man trotting over on an enormous horse. He seemed to be having trouble controlling it.

"Ah, Burns!" he boomed. "All set? Looking forward to the battle, eh?"

"I was," sighed Dad. "When do we start?"

"Not long," said the man. "We'll be on the right flank, defending the hill with Prince Percy. Pikemen at the front, of course."

Bertie raised his hand. "Where do I go?" he asked.

"Oh, this is my son, Bertie," explained Dad. "This is Sir Harry Crackpot, General of the King's infantry."

"I'm the King's drummer," said Bertie, thumping his drum.

Dirty Bertie

"Ha ha! Excellent!" wheezed Sir Harry, as his horse took him round in circles. "Well, you keep with me. We'll be guarding the King's flag."

"Can I fire the cannon?" asked Bertie.

"I don't think so!" chuckled Sir Harry. "Just stick with me. After they charge, I'm afraid we're out of the game."

"What game?" said Bertie.

"The battle, we're all killed. Didn't your dad tell you?"

"It's the battle of Bodge Hill," Dad explained. "The Roundheads win."

"Isn't that us?" said Bertie.

"No, we're the Royalists. We lose. Most of us end up dead."

Bertie frowned. "But I want to win!"

"Oh no, we can't win! Ha ha!" chuckled Sir Harry. "That wouldn't be history."

Bertie looked confused. It made no sense. What was the point of fighting a battle if you weren't trying to win? In any case, there was no way he was going to lie down and die just because it was history.

CHAPTER 4

BAM BAM! BOOM! BAM BAM!

The Royalist army set off marching up the hill. Sir Harry rode at the front with the King's flag bearer marching behind. Next came Bertie, beating his drum. Once, he dropped his drumstick and almost got trampled by a line of pikemen. At the top of the hill, he had

Dirty Bertie

a great view of the battlefield. The
Roundhead army was drawn up in front
of the tents. The King's army held the hill
with the royal flag waving in the wind.

Sir Harry Crackpot made a long
speech. Bertie beat his drum till he
felt his arms were going to drop off.
Then the two armies yelled insults at
each other from a safe distance. Bertie
thought it was a funny sort of battle.
When were they going to get on with
the fighting?

BOOM!

A cannon thundered in the distance,
sending out a puff of grey smoke. *At
last, this is more like it*, thought Bertie.
The Roundhead army charged, waving
their swords and cheering. Some of
them fell over.

Dirty Bertie

"This is it, men, hold your line!" yelled Sir Harry, his horse facing the wrong way.

Bertie beat his drum. He wished he had his pirate cutlass so he could fight the rotten Roundheads. Down the hill he could see Dad struggling with his pike as the enemy came into view. The two

Dirty Bertie

sides met in a giant rugby scrum at the foot of the slope. Swords clashed. People cried out. Smoke filled the air. When it cleared Bertie saw a lot of the King's men were lying down, either dead or having a nap. But the enemy carried on swarming up the hill.

Dirty Bertie

Bertie looked round. Sir Harry had fallen off his horse and was lying on his back. The King's flag lay forgotten in the mud. Bertie picked it up.

"No!" hissed Sir Harry urgently. "Put it down! We're all DEAD!"

"I'm not!" said Bertie. "I'm fine."

Three big Roundheads came up the hill with their swords drawn.

"You!" shouted the captain. "Hand over the flag!"

"No chance!" Bertie yelled back.

"Surrender!" ordered the captain.

"Surrender yourself!" said Bertie.

The Roundheads looked at each other. Their orders were to capture the King's flag. No one had mentioned anything about a dirty-faced drummer boy.

62

Dirty Bertie

Bertie's dad appeared out of the smoke. He was out of breath and missing his helmet.

"Bertie, it's okay," he panted. "Let them have it! It's all part of the battle."

Bertie shook his head stubbornly. "It's the King's flag."

"I know. That's the point. We lost."

"*I* haven't lost," said Bertie. "Not yet."

Dirty Bertie

The captain drew a long pistol and pointed it at him. "Bang! You're dead!" he said.

Bertie laughed. "You missed!" he cried.

The captain advanced, grimly. "Give me the flag, you little fool!"

Bertie shook his head. He raised the flagpole and brought it down on his opponent's helmet.

BASH!

Dirty Bertie

"OWWW!" cried the captain,
clutching his head. "Right, that's it. We're
not messing about now, hand it over
or else."

Bertie backed away. He was
outnumbered three to one. Suddenly he
had a brainwave.

"Look!" he shouted, pointing down the
hill. "The King!"

The three Roundheads turned round
to look. Bertie seized his chance and
set off running like the wind. Down
the slope he found more rotten
Roundheads blocking his way. He
weaved in and out of them, dodging
their attempts to wrestle him to the
ground.

"STOP THAT BOY!" yelled the
captain. "Don't let him get away!"

Dirty Bertie

But Bertie was too quick for them. In an instant he was racing across the battlefield, the royal flag streaming out in the wind. About fifty Roundheads gave chase, puffing and panting as they tried to catch up.

Dad stood with Sir Harry, watching them from the hill.

"Good Lord!" said the general. "I'm not sure it's history."

"No," said Dad, picking up his pike, "but I know someone who'll be history when I get hold of him."

CHAPTER 1

Miss Boot didn't often look pleased, but today she was smiling – or at least not scowling.

There was a reason for this. Last week Swotter House School had got their picture in the paper again. Usually, this made Miss Boot green with envy – they were always winning awards or meeting some important person. But this time it had given her an idea. It was high time Pudsley Junior got their name in the paper, and she knew how.

"Can anyone tell me what this is?" she asked.

"A book!" shouted Darren.

"Don't call out please, Darren. What kind of book?"

Know-All Nick shot up his hand. "*The Bumper Book of Records*, Miss."

"I've got that book," cried Bertie. "It's fantastic!"

"Thank you, Bertie," said Miss Boot. "This is a special book all about setting records. A record is something that no one has done before."

"Like when Bertie locked Mr Grouch in the shed?" asked Darren.

Dirty Bertie

"No, not like that," scowled Miss Boot. "A record is when you run faster or jump higher than anyone else. Now, I've talked to Miss Skinner and we think our school should try to set a record."

The class gasped. Bertie was so excited he almost fell off his chair. He had always wanted to set a world record – and he bet he could do it, too. Imagine it – his name in *The Bumper Book of Records*:

"The loudest burp of all time was recorded by schoolboy Bertie Burns. Bertie's burp was so loud it cracked his teacher's glasses and was heard 100 miles away in Manchester."

Dirty Bertie

He would be famous. He would be interviewed on radio and TV. People would pay millions of pounds just to hear his record burp.

"So we need ideas," said Miss Boot. "What kind of record should we try to set?"

Hands waved in the air. Bertie's was the first to go up.

"Yes, Trevor," said Miss Boot.

"The highest bounce on a trampoline," said Trevor.

Miss Boot pulled a face. "Too dangerous."

"The longest tap dance," said Donna.

"Hmm, I'm not sure we've got *that* long," said Miss Boot.

Bertie's arm stretched higher. "Ooh, Miss, I know, Miss!"

"Yes, all right, Bertie," sighed Miss Boot.

"Burping!" cried Bertie.

"What?"

"Burping! I can burp really loud, ask anyone!"

Miss Boot rolled her eyes. "You cannot set a record for burping," she said.

"Why not? What about the longest burp ever?" asked Bertie. "With a bit of practice I bet I can burp for a whole minute. All I need is fizzy orange and—"

"NO, BERTIE!" snapped Miss Boot. "We are not doing anything to do with burping! Now does anyone have a sensible suggestion?"

Nisha raised her hand. "We could make a penny pyramid," she said.

Miss Boot looked interested. "A penny pyramid? Is that possible?"

Nisha nodded. "I've seen a picture. You need lots and lots of pennies."

"And where would we get them?"

"Collect them," said Nisha.

Miss Boot fingered her double chin. It might work, and it would fit in with their history work on Ancient Egypt. Better still, they were bound to get their picture in *The Pudsley Post*. It was so simple it was brilliant.

Dirty Bertie

"Nisha, I think that's a splendid idea,"
beamed Miss Boot. "Why don't we start
collecting pennies right away? Whoever
collects the most will win a prize."

Bertie groaned loudly. A penny
pyramid? Yawnsville! What was exciting
about that? If they had to make a
pyramid why not use something
interesting – like slugs?
Or even teachers?
You could stack
them on top
of each other
with Miss
Boot at the
bottom.

CHAPTER 2

That evening, Bertie explained Miss Boot's idea over supper.

"A penny pyramid?" said Dad. "What on earth is that?"

"Don't ask me," grumbled Bertie. "Miss Boot says we need to collect thousands of pennies, and whoever collects the most wins a prize."

Dirty Bertie

"Have you looked in your money box?" asked Mum.

"It's empty," said Bertie. "I was sort of hoping you might help."

Dad sighed. He dug in his pocket while Mum fetched her purse. They emptied all their pennies on to the table.

"Eleven!" said Bertie, when he'd counted them. "Is that all you've got?"

"I think the word you're looking for is 'thank you'," said Dad icily.

"Oh yeah, um thank you," said Bertie. If he was going to win the prize he'd need a lot more than eleven measly pennies.

"You won't break the record anyway," sneered Suzy. "It'd have to be a huge pyramid. You'd need millions of pennies."

Bertie pushed his baked beans around the plate. Suzy was right. It was pointless. How were they ever going to collect enough pennies? It was Miss Boot's fault. Why couldn't she have picked something interesting – like the record for eating baked beans. He'd be good at that.

"How fast do you reckon I can eat these beans?" he asked.

Mum sighed. "I've no idea."

"Go on, how fast?"

"Bertie, just eat your dinner, it's not a race!"

"But say it was – say this was the World Baked Bean Eating Championship,"

78

Dirty Bertie

said Bertie. "How fast do you think I could do it?"

Dad groaned. "We *don't* care!"

"Time me," said Bertie, setting down his knife and fork. Just see how long it takes. Ready… GO!"

He grabbed his plate, opened his mouth and tipped down the beans in one go.

SLURP!

Dirty Bertie

"Finished!" he said, licking his lips. Tomato sauce dribbled down his chin and plopped on the table.

"EWWW! That's disgusting!" complained Suzy. "Mum, tell him!"

"That's disgusting, Bertie," said Mum. "Use your fork."

"It takes too long," said Bertie. "How quick was that?"

"We weren't timing you!" said Dad.

"About ten seconds," said Bertie. "I bet that's a world record!"

After supper, Bertie went in search of his copy of *The Bumper Book of Records*. It turned out the record for eating a tin of baked beans was under seven seconds. That was incredibly fast. It would take him longer than that to get the tin open. Bertie flicked through the

pages of the book. The world's tallest
man, the longest toenails, the deadliest
snake, the fastest dog on a skateboard...
Wait! What was that again?

*"The fastest skateboarding dog is Tillman
the bulldog from California, USA. Tillman
skateboarded 100 metres across a car
park in 19.678 seconds."*

Bertie stared at the picture. A dog on
a skateboard – why had he never
thought of that before? It was brilliant –
the greatest record ever! Much better
than making a stupid
pyramid out of
pennies. He still
had his skateboard
in the shed. All he
needed now was
Whiffer.

CHAPTER 3

Two weeks later, the day of Pudsley
Junior's world record attempt arrived.
Bertie walked to school with Whiffer on
a lead and his skateboard jammed into
his backpack. He explained his genius
idea to Darren and Eugene on the way.

"What about your mum?" asked
Darren. "How did you persuade her to

Dirty Bertie

let you bring Whiffer to school?"

"Simple," said Bertie. "I told her that it was Bring your Pet to School day."

"And she believed you?" said Darren amazed.

Bertie nodded.

"But what if Miss Boot sees him?" said Eugene. "Dogs aren't allowed in school."

"She won't," said Bertie. "We'll smuggle him into the book cupboard before the bell goes."

"What if he barks?" objected Eugene.

"He won't. I've brought him some dog food," said Bertie. "Anyway, it's not for long, only till we go outside."

Eugene shook his head. "You're mad, Bertie! Miss Boot will go up the wall!"

"Well, I think it's a great idea," said

Darren. "Just think, we'll be famous! The world's fastest skateboarding dog!"

Eugene glanced at Whiffer doubtfully. "You think he can do it?"

"Of course he can," said Bertie. "He's been practising all week. Trust me, this will work!"

After the register, Miss Boot inspected the pennies her class had collected.

"Hands up anyone who has collected fifty or more?" she asked.

Almost every hand went up. Bertie groaned. He'd only collected twenty-four and most of those came from his gran.

"More than a hundred?" asked Miss Boot. "More than five hundred?"

Royston Rich was the only one left

Dirty Bertie

with his hand up.

"Well done, Royston!" said Miss Boot.
"You're the winner! How many pennies
did you collect?"

Royston heaved a sack on to
the table. "Two thousand,"
he said.

"Two thousand?"

"It was easy," said
Royston smugly.
"My dad went to
the bank and
changed a twenty
pound note."

"Oh," said Miss Boot.
"Well, here's your prize. Perhaps you
can start your own penny collection
with this." Royston stared glumly at the
Peter Rabbit Money Box.

Miss Boot collected in all the pennies and divided them into buckets. She explained that they would be building the penny pyramid out in the playground. Everyone would have a chance to take part.

"And we have some special visitors," she said. "*The Pudsley Post* is sending a photographer to take our picture. Not only that, but someone is coming from *The Bumper Book of Records.*"

The class cheered excitedly.

"WOOF!" barked Whiffer in the book cupboard.

Miss Boot frowned. "What was that?"

"Um … it was me," said Bertie. "I've got a cough."

Miss Boot narrowed her eyes. "It sounded like a dog."

"Yes, it's a barking cough," said Bertie.
"Woof woof!"

Miss Boot scowled. "Well, don't cough
over anyone else," she said. "Right,
everyone line up at the door."

Bertie breathed out. It was a close
thing, but he'd got away with it.

CHAPTER 4

Outside, the penny pyramid gleamed in the sun. They had begun by laying hundreds of pennies in a square to act as the base. Then each layer had to be added carefully on top, getting smaller to create the shape of a pyramid. It was a delicate task. One slip and the whole pile would come crashing down.

Dirty Bertie

They had been working for three hours in the sun. The children stood patiently waiting their turn. Miss Boot had forbidden them to run, make a noise or even whisper. *The Pudsley Post* photographer took pictures while the woman from *The Bumper Book of Records* filmed on her camcorder.

Bertie peeped round the side of the school.

"You're sure this is a good idea?" whispered Eugene.

"Stop worrying!" said Bertie.

"Yeah, it's going to be great," said Darren.

Bertie was certain Whiffer would rise to the occasion. After all, if Tillman the bulldog could ride a skateboard, any dog could do it.

Dirty Bertie

"Okay, let's go," he whispered. The three of them crept out from their hiding place. Bertie kept a close eye on Miss Boot, who luckily had her back to them. He hauled Whiffer on to the skateboard and took off his lead. It took three or four attempts to get him to stay on. He kept climbing off or facing the wrong way. But at last they got him standing in position.

Dirty Bertie

"Ready?" whispered Bertie. "When I say 'go' we'll push him off."

Eugene nodded and set the timer on his watch.

Whiffer didn't look thrilled to be attempting the world doggie skateboarding record. His crash helmet had slipped down over one eye and he was chewing the strap.

Miss Boot was helping Trevor to lay the next step of pennies. A few more and the pyramid would be finished. Bertie started the countdown.

"Three, two, one … GO!" he yelled.

They launched the skateboard with a mighty push. Whiffer gave a yelp as it went zooming across the playground. His ears flapped like a pair of windsocks.

Dirty Bertie

"Uh oh," said Bertie.

Miss Boot had turned round – just in time to see a skateboarding dog hurtling towards her at the speed of light. For a moment she thought she must be dreaming. She stepped in front of the precious pyramid to try and prevent disaster.

Dirty Bertie

"NO, STOP! STOP!" she yelled, waving her arms.

Whiffer couldn't stop, he only knew it was time to get off. He leaped into Miss Boot's arms. The skateboard zoomed on by itself.

"NOOOOOO!" yelled Miss Boot, tottering backwards.

Dirty Bertie

CRASH!

Bertie hid his eyes. When he looked again Whiffer was standing on Miss Boot's chest. The class stared in horror. There were thousands of pennies scattered all over the playground.

Miss Boot pushed Whiffer off and staggered to her feet. She glared round, breathing hard. There was only one person who could have done this, and there he was trying to sneak away.

"BERTIE!" she roared. "COME HERE!"

Bertie turned round. "It wasn't my fault," he mumbled.

Miss Boot stomped towards him, purple with fury.

"LOOK!" she raged. "ALL OUR HARD WORK! WASTED! BECAUSE OF YOU!"

"I can explain," gulped Bertie.

"We might have broken the record," Miss Boot stormed. "Our picture would have been in the paper! You've ruined everything!"

"Not *everything*," mumbled Bertie. "We could always start again?"

Dirty Bertie

"START AGAIN?" screamed Miss Boot. "That took us nearly FOUR HOURS!"

"Okay," said Bertie. "I've got another idea."

Miss Boot's eyes blazed. "For your sake, Bertie, it had better be good."

"It is," said Bertie. "You'll love it. All we need is a lot of fizzy orange!"